Acting Edition

Some the Rain, Sometimes the Sea

by Julia Izumi

‖ SAMUEL FRENCH ‖

FOR PRODUCTION INQUIRIES

UNITED STATES AND CANADA
info@concordtheatricals.com
1-866-979-0447

UNITED KINGDOM AND EUROPE
licensing@concordtheatricals.co.uk
020-7054-7298

Each title is subject to availability from Concord Theatricals Corp., depending upon country of performance. Please be aware that *SOMETIMES THE RAIN, SOMETIMES THE SEA* may not be licensed by Concord Theatricals Corp. in your territory. Professional and amateur producers should contact the nearest Concord Theatricals Corp. office or licensing partner to verify availability.

No one shall make any changes in this title(s) for the purpose of production. No part of this book may be reproduced, stored in a retrieval system, scanned, uploaded, or transmitted in any form, by any means, now known or yet to be invented, including mechanical, electronic, digital, photocopying, recording, videotaping, or otherwise, without the prior written permission of the publisher. No one shall share this title(s), or any part of this title(s), through any social media or file hosting websites.

For all inquiries regarding motion picture, television, online/digital and other media rights, please contact Concord Theatricals Corp.

MUSIC AND THIRD-PARTY MATERIALS USE NOTE

Licensees are solely responsible for obtaining formal written permission from copyright owners to use copyrighted music and/or other copyrighted third-party materials (e.g. artworks, logos) in the performance of this play and are strongly cautioned to do so. If no such permission is obtained by the licensee, then the licensee must use only original music and materials that the licensee owns and controls. Licensees are solely responsible and liable for clearances of all third-party copyrighted materials, including without limitation music, and shall indemnify the copyright owners of the play(s) and their licensing agent, Concord Theatricals Corp., against any costs, expenses, losses and liabilities arising from the use of such copyrighted third-party materials by licensees. For music, please contact the appropriate music licensing authority in your territory for the rights to any incidental music.

IMPORTANT BILLING AND CREDIT REQUIREMENTS

If you have obtained performance rights to this title, please refer to your licensing agreement for important billing and credit requirements.

SOMETIMES THE RAIN, SOMETIMES THE SEA was first produced by Brown University's Sock & Buskin in Providence, RI, on April 5, 2018. It was directed by Kate Bergstrom and assistant directed by Ahmed Ashour, with set design by Renee Suprenant, assistant set design by Zach Silberberg, costume design by Alison Walker Carrier, lighting design by Tim Hett, sound design by Noah Usher, and props design by Miranda Friel. The production stage manager was Jessie Zambrano. The cast was as follows:

RAIN CLOUD	Karishma Swarup
BESSIE	Anthony DeRita
RALMOND	Kai Barshack
MIDI	Marianne Verrone
EDVARD	Conor Sweeney
INA	Oyindamola Akingbile
DOLAN	Brendan Geroge
LITTLE ONE	Maaike Laanstra-Corn

SOMETIMES THE RAIN, SOMETIMES THE SEA was first professionally produced by Rorschach Theatre (Jenny McConnell Frederick and Randy Baker, Artistic Directors) at Atlas Theater in Washington, D.C., on March 27, 2023. It was directed by Gregory Keng Strasser, with set design by Sarah Beth Hall, costume design by Alexa Cassandra Duimstra, lighting design by Dean Leong, sound design by Veronica J. Lancaster, video design by Hailey LaRoe, and props design by Rooster Skylar Sultan. The production stage manager was Caraline Jeffrey. The cast was as follows:

RAIN CLOUD	Sydney Dionne
BESSIE	Arika Thames
RALMOND	Jordan Brown
MIDI	Janine Baumgardner
EDVARD	Colum Goebelbecker
INA	Jordanna Hernandez
DOLAN	Nick Martin
LITTLE ONE	Jolene Mafnas

CHARACTERS

RAIN CLOUD *(pronounced like* 🌧️ *)*
No age / A rain cloud, then a female human

BESSIE *(pronounced like* 🐑 *?)*
Age unknown / A cow? A sea witch? A human? A dream?

RALMOND *(pronounced like "almond" with an R in front)*
28, then no age / A male human, then a rain cloud

MIDI *(pronounced like "mini" but with a D in the middle)*
29 / A female human

EDVARD *(pronounced like "Edward" with a V in the middle)*
Just Old Enough to Marry / A royal male human

INA *(pronounced like "I? Nah.")*
Old Enough to Marry / A secretly royal female human

DOLAN *(pronounced like "Dole Whip"* * *except instead of "whip" you say "an")*
Timeless / Hans Christian Andersen

LITTLE ONE *(NOT pronounced like "mermaid")*
Little / A female hero and storyteller

SETTING

A far off city where rain clouds fall in love with humans

A far off kingdom where mermaids fall in love with humans

A far off past where humans fall in love with humans

RULE

Dolan cannot physically touch any of his characters, so he often stays as far away as possible. His characters have the ability to touch him, and when they do it feels like water and knives.

---

* A Dole Whip is a simple yet delectable dessert sold exclusively in Disney World and Disneyland.

CASTING

While all the characters speak as people in Hans Christian Andersen's real life, they do not look anything like them (or else Dolan would recognize them!). This play is about overturning old narratives and takes place in fantastical realms. If your fantasy world is populated mostly by people who look like they walked out of eighteenth-century Denmark, then I recommend you choose a different play. It is particularly necessary for the narrative for Rain Cloud, Ralmond, and Ina to be played by actors of mixed race and/or who are immigrants of color or children of immigrants of color. There is even more resonance in the narrative if Rain Cloud is played by an actor of Indian descent. The name "Midi" is actually short for "Midori" which is the Japanese word for green (like the grass), if that also informs anything. Bessie is a female cow but can be played by an actor of any gender—Bessie takes ownership of gender fluidity in a way that Hans Christian Andersen could not.

In loving memory of Travis Johnson

(Somewhere, it is raining.)

VOICE.   Beyond the tallest buildings
And the highest mountains,
The sky is as vast as the imagination.

And way up above,
When a breath meets a breath,
They form a cloud.

And when the clouds collect close
They turn grayer than the thickest stone.
And become rain clouds.

Now on one occasion, three breaths uniquely met
And something happened that hadn't before:
A rain cloud was formed with a soul.

*(***RAIN CLOUD*** appears.)*

This Rain Cloud was unlike any other
For this Rain Cloud could see the world below
And think about the world below
And the Rain Cloud
Wanted to know
More
About the trees
And the grass
And the cows

(A cow moos in the distance.)

VOICE.   And especially about

          The humans

          Where they went

          How they went

          And why they hid underneath those awful sheets on sticks.

          (**RAIN CLOUD** *goes "blegh."*)

          One particular human caught the Rain Cloud's attention.

          This human was particular in three ways.

RAIN CLOUD. One...

VOICE.   He held no umbrella in his hands.

RAIN CLOUD. Two...

VOICE.   In fact his hands were empty and outstretched, as if he welcomed the rain.

RAIN CLOUD. Three...

VOICE.   And most importantly, he faced not down, not forward, but up.

          And the Rain Cloud saw his eyes.

          And the Rain Cloud thought:

RAIN CLOUD & VOICE. One and Two and Three

     He is made for me.

VOICE.   And as for the human—

          (**RALMOND** *appears, arms outstretched, looking up.*)

          He was not really thinking or seeing or learning.

          Only feeling.

And slowly some words escaped him on a breath:

RALMOND. I love the rain.

VOICE. And when that breath collided with a raindrop—

(It stops raining.)

*(**RAIN CLOUD** falls into **RALMOND**'s arms.)*

(Like plops from the sky, crash landing in his arms.)

RALMOND. Oh god, oh god, what happ— are you okay?

RAIN CLOUD. Oh god, oh god, what happ— are you okay?

RALMOND. I'm fine, but you—?!

RAIN CLOUD. I'm fine, but you...?

RALMOND. Me?

RAIN CLOUD. Me...?

RALMOND. ...??

RAIN CLOUD. I love you.

RALMOND. *(Laughs awkwardly.)* Thanks. I'm. I'm gonna put you down now.

*(He gently and slowly tries to put **RAIN CLOUD** on the ground.)*

(It is supremely awkward. Limbs going in all directions.)

*(**RAIN CLOUD** doesn't quite know how to stand.)*

*(So it starts kind of tipping over and **RALMOND** has to hold it up.)*

Did you hurt your legs?

RAIN CLOUD. ...Legs. Cows have legs. I have legs?

RALMOND. Yeah?

RAIN CLOUD. I love you.

RALMOND. Thanks, I love...that you're still alive!

RAIN CLOUD. I am not a...live. I am a...Rain Cloud.

RALMOND. ...Oh?

RAIN CLOUD. I am a Rain Cloud. You love the rain. I love you.

RALMOND. Okay, so, um, I'm starting to get the feeling that "I love you" is not a hyperbolic statement of gratitude but a genuine feeling. So I'm gonna let you know that I do have a partner—a girlfriend. So, um, sorry.

RAIN CLOUD. You have a girlfriend. I have a cowfriend. You have legs. I have legs. You love me. I love—

RALMOND. No, no, you see, I don't love you—I can't love you because I have a girlfriend.

RAIN CLOUD. But I have a cowfriend and I love you.

RALMOND. Yes, but Midi and I have the kind of relationship where we love each other and nobody else.

RAIN CLOUD. What is a Midi?

RALMOND. A digital musical interface from the 80s. But also the name of my girlfriend.

RAIN CLOUD. Bessie is the name of my cowfriend. Midi is the name of your girlfriend. You are the name of my lovefriend.

RALMOND. No, *Ralmond* is the name of your lovefriend. No, wait, I mean—

RAIN CLOUD. *Ralmond* is the name of my lovefriend.

RALMOND. Boyfriend. Nope, wait, I mean—

RAIN CLOUD. Ralmond is the name of my *boyfriend*. And I have no name because I am a rain cloud. But I am a unique Rain Cloud. With a soul. That's what Bessie says. And Bessie is very wise.

RALMOND. You're a...rain cloud. With a soul...?

RAIN CLOUD. And you are a human. And all humans have souls.

RALMOND. Um, are you sure you don't want me to walk you somewhere?

RAIN CLOUD. I want you. I want you to love me.

RALMOND. *(A little blush.)* Right. I'm...I'm sorry that I... can't. Because of Midi. And because...because I am human! That's right, oh my god, yes, I'm a human! And I can only love other humans! That's it! That's why I can't love you!

RAIN CLOUD. Oh...

RALMOND. But! You seem like a really nice—!!

RAIN CLOUD. So if I become a human, then you will love me.

RALMOND. Uh...how would you...become a human?

RAIN CLOUD. I do not know. And when I do not know something, I go ask Bessie. I will go ask Bessie.

RALMOND. Cool, you go do that. Uh, see you around!

> **(RALMOND** *waves.)*

> **(RAIN CLOUD** *looks at its hand and copies the move back. A little intensely.)*

RAIN CLOUD. See! You! Around!

> **(RAIN CLOUD** *has returned to the sky.)*

> **(RALMOND** *rubs his eyes for there is no one there.)*

(It is raining again.)

*(**RALMOND** looks up at the rain.)*

RALMOND. Huh...

VOICE.   And there was thunder.

(Thunder. Lightning.)

Bessie was a cowfriend, and a very good one at that.

*(**BESSIE** moos.)*

Bessie moos at the rain

Giving Rain Cloud knowledge

And Rain Cloud waters the grass

Giving Bessie food

So Bessie and Rain Cloud liked each other very much.

As often friends do.

(Unless you are the kind of friends with weird tensions.)

*(**VOICE** laughs weirdly.)*

But in any case.

It is raining.

And there is thunder.

(Thunder. Lightning. Darkness.)

(It is raining.)

*(Lights up on **BESSIE**, a cow, sitting to tea with **RAIN CLOUD**.)*

*(Translations of **BESSIE**'s text are somehow communicated to the audience. The word "Translation" that precedes all her lines should be communicated as well.)*

RAIN CLOUD. But I must become a human, Bessie, because that is how Ralmond will love me and I love Ralmond. I love Ralmond, Bessie. I love Ralmond.

BESSIE. Moo. [Translation: I dunno, it's tricky...]

RAIN CLOUD. You must tell me how because Ralmond is made for me.

BESSIE. Moo... [Translation: Well...to become a human... A human must love you. And only you.]

RAIN CLOUD. But...Ralmond cannot love me unless I am a human...and you are saying I cannot become a human unless Ralmond loves me.

BESSIE. Moo. [Translation: That's why I said it's tricky, you dingdong.]

RAIN CLOUD. So then it is...not possible.

BESSIE. Moo. [Translation: Not "not possible." You can convince him to love your soul.]

RAIN CLOUD. My soul?

BESSIE. Moo. [Translation: Once he loves your soul, you will receive a human body. Then, he will love you as a human.]

(**BESSIE** *turns to the audience.*)

[To summarize, this story is saying that you cannot be a full human unless someone loves you.]

RAIN CLOUD & VOICE. Huh?(!)

BESSIE. *(Shrugs.)* Moo. [Translation: Lol, j/k.]

RAIN CLOUD. How can I make him love my soul?

BESSIE. Moo. [Translation: Moo.]

RAIN CLOUD. What?

BESSIE. Moo. [Translation: To moo is to make big gestures to show someone how much you love them.]

RAIN CLOUD. Gestures like this? I learned this from Ralmond.

(**RAIN CLOUD** *waves aggressively.*)

BESSIE. Moo… [Translation: I don't know how humans moo, but that's definitely not it.]

RAIN CLOUD. So I should study how humans moo and then moo Ralmond the way they do!

(**BESSIE** *laughs.*)

BESSIE. Moo moo! [Translation: Omg, did I say moo? I totally meant woo. My bad.]

RAIN CLOUD. Oh. I will *woo* Ralmond to make him love me!

BESSIE. Moo. [Translation: I mean it ain't gonna be easy because he loves a digital musical interface from the 80s.]

RAIN CLOUD. Won't wooing him make him stop loving Midi?

BESSIE. Moo moo moo. [Translation: Who knows, you know? Love is a very complicated concept. Like religion. And carbohydrates. But you better woo him quick before he seals the deal with something like marriage.]

RAIN CLOUD. Marriage?

BESSIE. Mooooo. [Translation: Marriage is committing to one human for life—which, like, I don't really understand, but apparently marriage can get you monogrammed towels. And once he is engaged to be married your soul will lose its purpose and you will dissolve into seafoam.]

RAIN CLOUD. (*Gasp.*) If I become seafoam, then I can never see you or Ralmond or anyone!

BESSIE. Moo. [Translation: But should that happen, know that I will always remember you.]

RAIN CLOUD. And I will always remember you, Bessie.

BESSIE. Moo! [Translation: Seriously, please don't forget me as you go ga-ga over this dude!]

RAIN CLOUD. I promise.

BESSIE. Moo. [Translation: Now, go get this Ralmond. If he's anything like an almond, he's probably very tasty.]

RAIN CLOUD. Thank you, Bessie. See you around!

(**RAIN CLOUD** *waves aggressively again.*)

BESSIE. Mooooo. [Translation: See you around, Rain Cloud.]

(**RAIN CLOUD** *runs off as* **BESSIE** *waves.*)

MOO! [Translation: Oh, dung, I forgot to warn about flooding—WAIT!]

VOICE.　　But the Rain Cloud had flown off.

Too soon to hear about the dangers of flooding.

Too eager to learn how the humans woo.

The Rain Cloud spends days above the people.

Watching them woo.

As the Rain Cloud lingers

There's water, water, everywhere.

Through the roofs, through the windows.

Best time to be a maintenance man.

Especially for leaky homes, like this one.

The home of Ralmond.

And Midi.

And there is thunder.

(*Thunder. Lightning. Darkness.*)

(*And, suddenly, when the lights come up, we are somewhere else.*)

(Instead of rain we can hear the sea.)

(And we happen upon **EDVARD** *in mid-speech to* **INA.***)*

EDVARD. —And you are all the sights worth seeing!

And all the songs worth singing!

And all the, the, the everything!

THE EVERYTHING!

Your eyes! Your lips! Your cheeks—! Do you know how incredible your cheeks are?!

Do people tell you how lucky they are to see you on a daily basis?

Because everyone who does not spend every moment of their time looking at you is wasting their life away.

Wasting.

WASTING!!!

You

Are

Necessary

To

Sea

Sky

Land

And

Me

And

Everything

And

I

Can't

I can't.

(Big breath.)

(Pause.)

Please say something.

INA. Okay. Bye.

EDVARD. Wait, did you—did you not—did you hear what I said?

INA. Yea.

EDVARD. Do you need me to say it again? I can start over—

INA. That's not necessary.

EDVARD. But I just, like, bore my soul to you and, like, I just feel like...you maybe didn't get that.

INA. Well... I asked you which way the seamstress was and I feel like you didn't get *that*. So...

(She starts to leave again but he cuts her off.)

EDVARD. But I think I'm in love with you!

INA. But I think you're crazy.

EDVARD. You don't believe in love at first sight?

INA. I don't believe you can know someone in a minute.

EDVARD. You know I'm crazy in a minute.

INA. I have evidence.

EDVARD. I have evidence too! In my body!

INA. Excuse me?!

EDVARD. That's not what I meant! I mean it's kind of what I meant. I mean I don't really know what I meant— Please, give me a chance! I'm good at music! And bowling!

INA. I hate bowling.

EDVARD. Me too!

INA. What?

EDVARD. I'm sorry, I have, like, zero control of what is coming out of my mouth right now please help me. Or kill me. No seriously. Killing me would really help me out right now.

(*She chortles.*)

You think I'm funny.

INA. I think you need help.

EDVARD. I'm just impulsive.

INA. That's not good for a future king.

(*Pause. Oops.*)

EDVARD. So. You know who I am.

INA. Your face is on many things, in case you haven't noticed.

EDVARD. I'm disguised.

INA. How?

EDVARD. I'm wearing a hat.

INA. Everyone can still see your face.

EDVARD. Well, no one else has ever talked to me!

INA. They don't want to talk to you, they just want to look at you. People don't want to treat royal humans like humans. They want to admire them like statues.

EDVARD. So you're calling me a work of art.

INA. I'm calling you an idiot if you think that's a compliment.

EDVARD. An idiot you were looking at.

INA. I was looking for the seamstress! I'm still looking for the seamstress!

EDVARD. You really thought that I, a royal human, who has a royal tailor, would know where the local seamstress was?

INA. A good royal human knows everything about their kingdom.

EDVARD. Or maybe. You thought you kinda fell in love with me. I mean, a lot of people do, I am a prince. And you saw me today and you thought, "Maybe." Maybe if you casually talked to me and pretended like you didn't know who I was, then I would fall in love with you. Because you didn't see the royal human, you saw a human. And that would get me, that would...really get me... But I see you too! And I see what you're doing! I gotcha! Oh my god you're blushing—I'm right, aren't I?

(Silence.)

INA. You're an ass.

(She starts to go.)

EDVARD. Wait! I'm so sorry—If you could give us a chance to get to know each other, then I promise—

INA. I don't owe you anything.

EDVARD. You would disobey royalty?

INA. Are you threatening me?

EDVARD. Yes! Maybe! No! I dunno! Feelings are hard! Please just...let me ask one thing about you, and then I promise to...never speak to you again.

INA. Promise?

EDVARD. Yes.

*(**INA** stares at him for a moment.)*

INA. Fine.

EDVARD. Okay. What is your...biggest fear?

INA. ...Drowning.

> *(Pause.)*

May I ask you a question?

EDVARD. Please!

> *(**INA** walks up to **EDVARD**, eyes locked, slowly.)*
>
> *(Once her face is super duper close to his...)*

INA. Which way is the seamstress?

EDVARD. ...Two streets that way, then make a left. Third house on the right.

INA. ...Thank you.

> *(She stomps on his foot. Hard.)*
>
> *(**INA** walks away.)*
>
> *(**EDVARD** is in so much pain but he is smiling. He hobbles off in the opposite direction.)*
>
> *(Then, **DOLAN** weirdly enters. **DOLAN** is a thin, tall, gawkward [gawky and awkward] man and the owner of the previous **VOICE**. He holds a book.)*

DOLAN. ...Hi.

...

...

Um...hello.

Hi.

I'm.................................Dolan.

And I'm a very famous and very genius storyteller

Who has been blessing you all

With this brand new story

That I created

Called:
The Little Rain Cloud.

I didn't mean to interrupt my lovely little story—
And I wouldn't interrupt unless it was utterly necessary—
But I do need to make something very clear:
That scene that just happened.
Is not a scene from *The Little Rain Cloud.*
I don't know what that was or where that came from
or who those strange but very beautiful people were...
But they are not part of my brilliant new story.

So.
Obviously the way to fix this
Is for us all to simply
Forget
That any of this happened.
On the count of three
That scene will just
~Disappear~
from your minds.
Ready?

One.
Two.
Three!

    (He does some kind of odd gesture.)

There. All gone!
Now we can return to my story.

    (He starts exiting, but he comes back.)

I hope you're liking it, by the way.
I'm a very famous writer so you should.

> (**DOLAN** *starts exiting again, but comes back again.*)

DOLAN. And you know, if you don't like it
Or if you think it's "childish" or "outdated" or "problematic"
Then maybe that's a problem with *you*,
Because as I said,
I am a genius
And ergo
So is my story.

> (*He barely exits again before he comes straight back.*)

And you know.
I didn't just become a genius overnight.
I was born this way.
I came into this world with so much talent
They didn't know what to do with me.
I tried many different paths for my genius to shine.
In fact, I could have been a famous, genius actor
But then I went to get an education
And became a famous, genius writer instead.
So. You're welcome.

> (*He's getting very comfy center stage now.*)

And with all my genius, I know what you are thinking:
How could anyone, anywhere
Possibly think my glorious stories
Are "childish" or "outdated" or "problematic"?
And the truth is
They don't!
But!

We are in wild, ~contemporary~ times
Where there are allegedly some ~contemporary~ people
Who may occasionally have these erroneous thoughts
about my genius work.
So I've written this new story to prove
That I am
Timeless.

Truly, how can these *critics*—
Or ~haters~
(See I can be very ~contemporary~)
Say that my works are
"Juvenile"
Or "Of another time"
Or "Not reflective of our current values"
When they have always been about my values
And my values
Are the values
Of
GOD.

    (He laughs weirdly.)

But that's enough about...me.
Let's return to *The Little Rain Cloud*!
Where were we—

    (Looks in book.)

Yes! Maintenance men!
Thrilling time to be one!

       Because some homes have little leaks.

       And some homes have little floods.

       And some homes have both, like this one.

DOLAN.   The home of Ralmond.

And Midi.

(Isn't she pretty?)

(Clears throat.)

And there is thunder.

(Thunder. Lightning.)

(Lights up on Ralmond and Midi's apartment.)

(There are buckets everywhere, catching drops of water.)

(And the floor is covered in soaked towels.)

*(**RALMOND** has a book open and sees **MIDI**, at the door.)*

(She is drenched, and holds a pile of completely demolished umbrellas.)

RALMOND. Midi! You're—soaked! I bought the last towel on the rack for us, let me grab it—

*(**RALMOND** puts his book on the table and runs off.)*

MIDI. Twenty-three.

RALMOND. *(Offstage.)* What?

MIDI. TWENTY-THREE! Twenty-three umbrellas I saw trashed on the street just on my way home.

*(**RALMOND** brings out a towel.)*

RALMOND. Here you go—

*(**RALMOND** spreads it out.)*

*(**MIDI** ignores it, grabs a pen and paper and sits on the couch.)*

(**RALMOND** *places the towel on her shoulders during the below.*)

MIDI. That counts for...maybe roughly 1 cubic foot of landfill when compressed—it's roughly a 1.2 mile walk home—so the whole city might have about 70 cubic feet worth of landfill in umbrellas—multiplied by the 7 days it has not stopped raining... yikes...

RALMOND. Midi...

MIDI. If the folks in the Sanitation Department would just put umbrellas on the posters for what's recyclable like I told them to the last time we had that storm, then maybe fewer people would just leave them on the street—when's my next meeting with them? Next Tuesday? No, Wednesday? Maybe I can ask to move it to Friday—ugh but Friday is the big meeting with the mayor about the unhoused population in the impending flood—

RALMOND. Midi—

MIDI. Maybe I can squeeze it in tomorrow? If it's still raining the site visit to the new communal garden might get cancelled—oh but I have to go tomorrow because that's the day the contractor is—

(**RALMOND** *grabs* **MIDI**'s *head and touches his forehead to hers.*)

(*They take a breath together.*)

RALMOND. Hi.

MIDI. Hi.

RALMOND. How are you, Midi?

MIDI. I'm...cold. How are you, Rallie?

RALMOND. I'm okay. I'm hungry. How was your day?

MIDI. So fun. I yelled at old men in suits about how the week of rain is proof of environmental destruction. How was your day?

RALMOND. Not bad. The gym is leaking so all the seventh graders were cranky. But I calmed them down with my natural charisma and authoritative presence.

MIDI. You showed them a movie?

RALMOND. Yup! It was actually perfect timing for my lesson plan. We're looking at fairytale adaptations and comparing them to the original text. It's been kinda cool—have you read the original *Little Mermaid*?

>   (**RALMOND** *shows* **MIDI** *the book he's reading.*)

>   (**DOLAN** *pokes his head in, like, "Wait, what?"*)

MIDI. Isn't *The Little Mermaid* like super problematic?

DOLAN. AUGH!

>   (**MIDI** *looks towards the window and* **DOLAN** *retreats.*)

MIDI. Isn't that story about a mermaid who gives up her voice and changes her entire body just to be loved by some man? *(Mocking voice.)* And then they all lived happily ever after...

RALMOND. Actually in the original story, it's not quite happily ever after... the Mermaid does give up her voice to the Sea Witch in exchange for a pair of legs, but she can only remain a human if the Prince decides to marry her. He ends up marrying a Princess who he thinks saved him from drowning in a shipwreck, even though it was actually the Little Mermaid who rescued him. On the night of the Prince's wedding, the Mermaid is given a choice: she can become body-less seafoam, or she can kill the Prince and go back to being a mermaid in the sea.

MIDI. So then she kills him! And she takes down the patriarchy!

RALMOND. *(Laughs.)* No!

MIDI. You're telling me that this mermaid not only changed who she was and lost her voice for this man who doesn't even love her back, but also sacrifices her life to save his?

RALMOND. Okay, maybe she's not the best role model but... she's in love, you know? People sacrifice a lot for love... And maybe, there's a way to think about her ending so that it's not just a sacrifice but...the best option for *her*. Maybe she didn't ever feel like she belonged in the sea as a mermaid. But when the Prince still doesn't love her back as a human, she realizes—she doesn't belong as a human either. So if there's a chance to become seafoam, maybe she thinks, "Hmm, I've never been seafoam before. That sounds kind of fun, why not give it a try!" Then maybe it's more a story about finding yourself than it is about—

MIDI. Rallie, I think you've put a little too much thought into this dated children's story.

RALMOND. Uh... yeah... yeah, maybe...

MIDI. I just don't understand why she couldn't have found another option. See, this is what I can't stand about fairytale characters, they are so swept up in their emotions that they don't think rationally. Although this week of straight rain has made me feel like I'm stuck in a fairytale. Maybe next I'll see a pumpkin turn into a coach!

RALMOND. *(Not quiet enough.)* Or a rain cloud turn into a person...

MIDI. Right, 'cause that would be your dream girl, Mr. No Umbrella. A person who is literal rain.

RALMOND. No. No it wouldn't. I would never—no—

MIDI. I need to shower and change before what I'm sure will end up becoming a five-hour strategy call.

RALMOND. Oh, I thought we were gonna—

MIDI. Shit! I totally said we would eat dinner together, didn't I? I'm so sorry, we had to cancel our staff meeting this morning because everyone's commutes got messed up with the rain and we have to start planning for Friday's meeting with the mayor...

RALMOND. ...That's okay. I'll keep the lasagna warm for you in the oven.

MIDI. Thank you... I am really, really sorry, Rallie.

RALMOND. It's okay. You're saving the world!

MIDI. I dunno about that... But don't worry, nobody is touching Saturday. I promise. Completely blocked off. Everything in my calendar. Just for us.

(*She kisses him on the cheek.*)

(*As she's exiting.*) Man, I hate the rain. I wish I could tell it to just leave us all alone.

RALMOND. I dunno, they're pretty stubborn...

(**RALMOND** *looks at his book.*)

(*He opens a page and starts to read aloud.*)

> "The Little Mermaid held the Prince's head above the water—

RALMOND & A DIFFERENT FEMALE VOICE.
> And let the waves drift them to the nearest shore
>
> As she stayed above, she couldn't help but look up
>
> She had never seen lightning so close,
>
> Or heard *thunder* so near—"

(*Thunder. Lightning.*)

(**DOLAN** *has been creeping out onstage during the above, looking for the* **DIFFERENT FEMALE VOICE**.)

DOLAN. No it's only when *I* say thunder—!!

(Darkness. When lights come back up, **RALMOND** *is gone, and, in his stead, there is* **INA** *over* **EDVARD***'s body on the floor.)*

*(***INA*** is listening for breath.)*

*(***DOLAN***, out of panic, crouches in a corner and watches.)*

INA. Please be alive, please be alive! I feel like you're not breathing, are you breathing? Am I breathing? I'm breathing. Good. Hold on. I'll um.

(She tries to drag him by the shoulders but it doesn't work.)

Okay, not working—um—Maybe I can go get someone to—oh, who the hell is going to believe me? "I found the Prince, unconscious and alone on a shore. No, I didn't try to kill him." *(Laughs to herself.)* This is not funny. I guess I can—um—just—wake up, please, wake up, and don't *(She grabs his face and pulls him close.)* —don't head to the light, okay? IF YOU SEE A LIGHT DON'T HEAD THERE, DON'T GO TO THE DEAD PLACE—

EDVARD. …Jesus—

*(***INA*** drops ***EDVARD*** and his head hits the floor.)*

Ow!

INA. Sorry! You freaked me out! I thought you were—

*(***INA*** and ***DOLAN*** breathe a sigh of relief.)*

(Then ***DOLAN*** *is like, "wait, why am I relieved?")*

Thank god you're all right—

DOLAN. And then out of nowhere, there was thunder!

(Thunder. Lightning. Darkness.)

*(Lights up on **DOLAN** alone.)*

DOLAN. Phew.

Hi. It's me, Dolan.
Remember me?

I'm so sorry.
That was also not a scene in *The Little Rain Cloud*.
I don't know what keeps happening.
Like.
What was that?
It seemed like that very handsome but cocky Prince character almost drowned and that beautiful fool of a woman found him and she's about to take all the credit for saving him, even though it was really this other mysterious being who saved him and loves this Prince character so much she's willing to give up her voice to be a...

...

...

...

(That weird laugh again.)

You know.
That storyline
May sound familiar to you.
Because it's from this very famous masterpiece.
But.
That's not what that inappropriate scene was from.
Because those people we just saw
Are DERANGED.
They are not in that other masterpiece.
And I should know.

Because I...

Have read that other famous story.

Many times.

Because it's so good.

I mean, really, who do those nutjobs think they are?!

Why were they being so attractive—

I mean annoying!!!

Definitely not the kind of people you would find in my stories.

Speaking of which:

> (**RAIN CLOUD** *appears.*)

> (**DOLAN** *recedes offstage.*)

>> The Rain Cloud was finally ready to woo Ralmond
>>
>> And one day.
>>
>> A Saturday to be exact.
>>
>> Ralmond stood still, with no umbrella, looking up.

> (**RALMOND** *appears.*)

>> And he let words slip, this time on a sigh:

RALMOND. I love the rain.

> (*It stops raining.*)

> (**RAIN CLOUD** *falls into* **RALMOND**'s *arms.*)

> (*This time maybe not so crazily? Or maybe even more crazily.*)

RAIN CLOUD. RALMOND!

RALMOND. HOW DO YOU DO THAT?!

> (**RAIN CLOUD** *hops off with ease this time.*)

RAIN CLOUD. Ralmond! I found you! Because I love you! Because you ARE meant for me!

RALMOND. Oh my god. *(Looks up.)* It stopped raining.

RAIN CLOUD. Yes I am here and not in the sky!

RALMOND. It's been raining for twelve days. And now you're here. And now it's stopped.

RAIN CLOUD. Yes, I have been learning how humans woo for twelve days. And now I have three actions to woo you.

RALMOND. What do you mean—?!

>   (**RAIN CLOUD** *puts its hand out to shush* **RALMOND.***)*

RAIN CLOUD. Shhh. Do not interrupt my wooing!

One.

>   (**RAIN CLOUD** *motions for* **RALMOND** *to put his hands out.)*
>
>   *(He does.)*
>
>   (**RAIN CLOUD** *places a pile of grass and trees and mud and maybe cowdung on* **RALMOND***'s hands.)*

This is the most important thing I have. I saw this in the store and I thought of you. I inherited this from my favorite aunt and I want you to have it. Happy Birthday. Happy Valentine's Day. Happy Anniversary. Congrats on getting the job. PLEASE I'LL GIVE YOU ANYTHING FOR THE LOVE OF GOD TAKE ME BACK YESSENIA PLEASE.* Happy Arbor Day.

Two.

>   (**RAIN CLOUD** *takes out a sheet of paper and pretends to "read" from it.)*

---

* This sentence can be replaced with a famous contemporary movie line that is a declaration of love.

Dear Ralmond,

Everyone who does not spend every moment of their time looking at you is wasting their life away.

Wasting.

WASTING!!!

You

Are

Necessary

To

Sea

Sky

Land

And

Me

And

Everything

And

I

Can't

I can't.

Love,

Rain Cloud

(That's me)

Three.

> (**RAIN CLOUD** *opens its mouth and out pours a siren song.**)
>
> (*It is so beautiful, so present, so penetrating, that it shakes the world.*)

---

* A license to produce *SOMETIMES THE RAIN, SOMETIMES THE SEA* does not include a performance license for any copyrighted music or recordings. Licensees should create their own. For further information, please see the Music and Third-Party Materials Use Note on page iii.

(Thunder. Lightning.)

DOLAN. What is happening?! What is this?!

(Perhaps amidst the lightning we see a silhouette of a mermaid swimming.)

(The noise transitions into **RAIN CLOUD** *singing.)*

*(**RAIN CLOUD** is a very bad singer.)*

RAIN CLOUD. And now I have finished wooing you and now you love me and we are lovers. Or partners. Or girlfriends. Or boyfriends. Or husbands. Or wives. Or beaus. Or boos. Or mistresses—and now we kiss.

*(**RAIN CLOUD** tries to kiss **RALMOND**.)*

RALMOND. Rain Cloud! Stop, we can't do that!

*(**RAIN CLOUD** is still advancing and **RALMOND** lifts **RAIN CLOUD** up to move it away.)*

Wow. I keep thinking it's the adrenaline when I catch you but... You really are as light as...a cloud. *(Laughs.)*

RAIN CLOUD. I am a cloud.

RALMOND. That's a joke. A joke is when...never mind, I'm not gonna mansplain jokes to you. But—thank you, Rain Cloud! I have honestly never been wooed. But... I love Midi.

RAIN CLOUD. Ralmond, I have seen people with girlfriends or boyfriends or partners who kiss many different people.

RALMOND. Yeah, but they're either in a different kind of relationship than I am, or they are breaking the rules. And you should live in an ideal world where rules are followed.

RAIN CLOUD. I do not want to live in an *ideal* world. I want to live in this world with you where I love you and you love me and we exist and be together. I want you. I love you.

RALMOND. Why, Rain Cloud? You barely know me.

RAIN CLOUD. One: You hate umbrellas. I hate umbrellas.

Two: You enjoy the rain. I am the rain.

Three: You see me...and you see me...and you...still see me. And that makes me feel...seen.

One and Two and Three

You were made for me.

RALMOND. Wow that's... yeah, okay, I guess, sure.

RAIN CLOUD. Why do you love Midi? Tell me so I can learn how to make you stop loving her.

RALMOND. *You* can't make me stop loving her.

RAIN CLOUD. Then how can I make you love me *more* than you love her?

RALMOND. Love...doesn't really work like that... it's complicated.

RAIN CLOUD. Like religion. And carbohydrates.

RALMOND. Not exactly... Let me try this: I could tell you a million reasons why I *like* Midi. She is thoughtful, passionate, she's constantly trying to save the Earth so she can save everyone in it—which is oddly something I sometimes don't like about her...

But I love her because...a shoelace.

I love her because a frying pan.

I love her because a tidal wave

I love her because an aftershave

RAIN CLOUD & DOLAN'S VOICE. What?(!!)

RALMOND. But, to be honest, sometimes...I wonder if she feels the same...

RAIN CLOUD. She doesn't love you?

RALMOND. She does...but sometimes I feel like...maybe it's different. But anyway, we'll see tonight. I'm gonna ask her to marry me.

RAIN CLOUD. No! Ralmond! Don't get a monogrammed towel!

RALMOND. What?!

RAIN CLOUD. I don't know what to do now! And when I do not know something I go ask Bessie—Ralmond, don't do anything until I come back or else I'll become seafoam!

> (**RAIN CLOUD** *returns to the sky.*)
>
> (*It starts raining again.*)
>
> (**RALMOND** *alone, confused and stunned.*)

RALMOND. Seafoam...like...*The Little Mermaid*?

> (**RALMOND** *looks down, at the increasing flood at his feet.*)

Oh crap... I think I figured out why it's flooding...

> (**DOLAN** *starts to creep out onstage.*)

DOLAN. Hi folks, apologies, I am not in this scene, I just have to give a little note—

(*To* **RALMOND**.) Hey you! Um, ~bro~, stop saying things I didn't write, yeah?

First talking about that unrelated fairytale and now this wonkadonk shoelace business—

You can't get away with anything just because you have a pretty face that anyone would want to forgive—

I forgive you—
No! Wait!

RALMOND. Midi!

DOLAN. No, no, not Midi—

RALMOND. You're early!

DOLAN. I'm Dolan.

RALMOND. You've never left work early in your life!

DOLAN. Listen to me, you gorgeous goof—

RALMOND. Did you bring *The Little Mermaid* with you?

DOLAN. *(Looks at his book.)* This? This is *The Little Rain Cloud*! I am trying to tell *The Little Rain Cloud*! Why is that so hard for people to understand!

RALMOND. I mean, I guess the writing is beautiful but—

DOLAN. You think so??

RALMOND. Of course. *(Shift.)* Everything you write is beautiful.

> *(Something changes.)*

DOLAN. You truly believe that, Harald?

RALMOND. *(As Harald.)* You don't need my praises to know how talented you are.

DOLAN. Well, if you think my writing is so beautiful, why did you burn my letters?

RALMOND. *(As Harald.)* ...Hans. I don't want Camilla to misunderstand them.

DOLAN. Misunderstand what? What harm is there in one man telling another his affection and—
Wait.
...
What is happening.

DOLAN. Aaaaand then there was thunder!

> *(Thunder. Lightning.)*

> *(**DOLAN** alone onstage.)*

Thank the lord and everything holy, that worked!

I'm so sorry, folks.

See, this is why I try not to enter the scenes.

I'm so charismatic that characters get confused.

Am I in them, am I not in them.

What's real, what's not real.

Who's Hans, who's not Hans.

What is a Hans, anyway?

There have been too many interruptions.

It's like someone doesn't want me to tell *The Little Rain Cloud…*

> *(He has an IDEA!)*

You know, since I'm already here

I'm gonna help with this next scene

Because why leave to amateurs that which you can do yourself?

~Bonus~

You folks are so lucky

Because this means

You get to see me do

A quick-change.

This is gonna be a real treat folks.

Ready?

> *(**DOLAN** puts on cow ears.)*

Tada!

It's me, Bessie.

Moo.

Just kidding it's me, Dolan.

But I had you fooled, didn't I?

Because I'm a very good actor.

> (**DOLAN** *prepares to be in the scene.*)

>> So Rain Cloud returns to Bessie in a panic,
>> Now understanding that Ralmond will
>> propose.

> (**RAIN CLOUD** *runs on.*)

RAIN CLOUD. Bessie! Ralmond is getting monogrammed towels—How can I make Midi break his heart?

DOLAN. Moo. Translation: You can't, you adorable acorn.

RAIN CLOUD. There must be a way, Bessie! He is made for me!

DOLAN. Moooo. Translation: Hmm, what if you save him before she does? Using your flood!

RAIN CLOUD. What is a flood?

DOLAN. A sea where—I mean, moo. Translation: A sea where there isn't supposed to be one. What if you almost drown Ralmond with your flood and then Midi doesn't save him, but you do? That would break his heart and make him love you.

RAIN CLOUD. …I don't want Ralmond to drown.

DOLAN. *(To audience.)* Folks, I'm just gonna do the translations, to speed this up. Hope that's all right with everyone—Although you don't have a choice because I'm the storyteller.

(To **RAIN CLOUD**.*)* He won't drown because you'll save him.

THE DIFFERENT FEMALE VOICE. Translation: Then stop flooding, Rain Cloud.

DOLAN. Come again?

THE DIFFERENT FEMALE VOICE. Translation: You're hurting the Earth with the flooding. You need to stop, Rain Cloud.

DOLAN. Um…sorry folks, there seems to be a glitch in the—

THE DIFFERENT FEMALE VOICE. Translation: If the Earth dies, so does the grass, and so does Bessie.

DOLAN. No, *I'm* Bessie!

THE DIFFERENT FEMALE VOICE. Translation: If you change your purpose from loving Ralmond to loving the Earth, you don't have to dissolve. You can be a rain cloud and water the Earth—just stop the flooding!

> *(During the above,* **DOLAN** *tries Mooing loudly to drown out the voice.)*

RAIN CLOUD. I don't understand what you're—

DOLAN. MOOOO! Translation: Drown him and save him! Okay? That's what you have to do to keep this story going in the direction it needs to! Yeah? Got it? Okay?

> *(A moment of tense silence where* **DOLAN** *is bracing himself for another translation.)*
>
> *(But it doesn't happen.)*

Thank Jesus. *(To audience.)* That was probably one of those ~haters~ trying to interrupt.

RAIN CLOUD. Thank you, Bessie.

DOLAN. Moo. Translation: You're welcome.

RAIN CLOUD. …What's a shoelace, Bessie?

DOLAN. …Huh?

RAIN CLOUD. Ralmond says he loves Midi because a... shoelace. What's a shoelace?

DOLAN. Holy Christ, do NOT listen to what that beautiful buffoon said.

RAIN CLOUD. Am I not in love, Bessie? If I don't know what that means?

DOLAN. Of course you're in love. It's very tragic because it's unrequited right now. But this is where the plot to almost drown him will—

RAIN CLOUD. No... I... I don't know if this is love.

DOLAN. Okay. Well. It is.

I wrote you.

And you are in love.

RAIN CLOUD. I feel like... *(Shift.)* you're forcing an idea of love on something that isn't.

(Something changes.)

DOLAN. It must be love! What else could there be but love between us, Louise?

RAIN CLOUD. *(As Louise.)* Affection. Deep understanding. Trust.

DOLAN. But our letters to each other are proof of our unbridled passion—

RAIN CLOUD. *(As Louise.)* I never said anything about passion, just a love that—

DOLAN. You must feel something for me, Louise, or else how could I be so tortured by you?

RAIN CLOUD. *(As Louise.)* As I said in my letters, my dear Hans Christian, I love you like a sister loves a brother not—

DOLAN. Wait! WAIT!

DOLAN. HOLY MARY, PUREST WOMAN TO HAVE LIVED GIVE ME THUNDER.

> *(Thunder. Lightning. Darkness.)*

> *(**DOLAN** alone.)*

Quickly, everyone, let's head to Midi and Ralmond's apartment before anything else—

> *(Lights up on the apartment where **EDVARD** is on the couch, eyes closed, with **INA** watching him intently. She is visiting him at the hospital.)*

No! No! Not you two captivating clowns!

Is someone doodling in my storybook?!

> *(He starts furiously flipping through the book.)*

INA. …Hey. …HEY!

> *(**EDVARD** open his eyes and is stunned.)*

…How are you?

EDVARD. …Horrible—

INA. I'll go get the nurse—

EDVARD. Because I know I can never again be as happy as I am right now, looking at you looking at me—

INA & DOLAN. OH MY GOD.

EDVARD. What?!

> *(**INA** throws a book or something at him.)*

INA. STOP THAT!!

EDVARD. STOP WHAT?!

INA. THIS THING YOU KEEP DOING!

EDVARD. WHAT THING?!

INA. I'M LEAVING!

> (**INA** *exits.*)

DOLAN. GET OUTTA HERE!

EDVARD. WAIT!

DOLAN. No no no don't wait!

> (**INA** *comes back.*)

EDVARD. WHAT'S YOUR NAME?!

INA. YOU JUST SPEW OUT BAD POETRY TO PEOPLE WHOSE NAMES YOU DON'T KNOW?!

EDVARD. I CAN'T HELP IT!!!!

INA. WELL HELP IT! I COULD BE A SERIAL KILLER!

EDVARD. ARE YOU?!

INA. ARE YOU SERIOUSLY ASKING ME IF I'M A SERIAL KILLER?!

DOLAN. It's a fair question!!!!!!!!!!!

EDVARD. I DUNNO!!! WHAT DO YOU WANT ME TO ASK!!

INA. I DON'T WANT YOU TO ASK ANYTHING!!!!

EDVARD. FINE!!

INA. FINE!!! GET WELL!!!!

> (**INA** *exits.*)

> (*But then she quickly returns.*)

MY NAME IS INA.

EDVARD. MY NAME IS—

INA. I KNOW YOUR DUMB NAME, PRINCE EDVARD.

DOLAN. ...Edvard?

> (**INA** *really exits.*)

No, no. That's not your name. That's not your name, right?

> (*But* **EDVARD** *cannot hear him. He is smiling to himself.*)

EDVARD. Ina... Ina...

DOLAN. What are we still doing here—THUNDER!

> (*Thunder. Lightning.*)

> (**EDVARD** *is gone.*)

I am so, so, SO sorry folks.

You came here to witness a heart-warming love story

And now it is a parade of bananas.

Why don't I just summarize everything that happens next so we can get to the good stuff?

So!

Midi stands Ralmond up.

Then Ralmond bursts into their apartment.

Midi is on all these phone calls.

And he proposes to her.

And they have this thunderous argument—

> (*Thunder. Lightning.*)

> (*When lights come up,* **RALMOND** *is on one knee, with a ring out.*)

> (**MIDI** *is indeed on many phone calls. There's also water everywhere.*)

MIDI. Rallie, this is seriously not the time—

RALMOND. You're not even gonna respond?!

MIDI. Do you see me right now? I am standing in water. WATER. In our own apartment. Think of what people without apartments are going through?!

RALMOND. It's a simple question. Will you marry me?

MIDI. There is literally a global crisis right now!

RALMOND. There is always going to be a global crisis!

DOLAN. Oh. My. Deviled. Eggs.

I was making a METAPHOR.
If you were a genius writer, you would understand!

Where are we?!

(**DOLAN** *flips through the pages of his book.*)

Oh, I found it!

This is my most sophisticated, dramatic scene.

(**DOLAN** *crouches in a corner of the scene.*)

MIDI. Please, can we table this?

RALMOND. I'm a human being, Midi, not a conversation to table. And—I know how to fix the flooding! There was a Rain Cloud with a soul who was in love with me, and it was wooing me all over the place, and that's why it was raining like crazy, but I'll tell it to leave so it's gonna stop raining.

MIDI. Rallie...are you all right? Do we need to go to the doctor or something—

RALMOND. I don't want to go to a doctor. I want to live in this world with you where I love you and you love me and we exist and be together. I want you. I love you.

MIDI. ...I think this rain is getting to all of us and making us say and do things that are not rational—

RALMOND. You couldn't even say it.

MIDI. Say what?

RALMOND. "I love you, too."

        (**RALMOND** *exits.*)

MIDI. Wait. Rallie. Rallie! Wait!

Shit.

        (*She starts picking up the calls.*)

Mayor Howell, I am so terribly sorry but I have to call you back—

DOLAN. (*Overlap.*) And now after that very intense and dramatic moment, we can move on to the—

MIDI. Rallie?

DOLAN. Dolan.

MIDI. Oh, thank god you came back. I didn't want us to end on a misunderstanding.

DOLAN. Yes, there is a misunderstanding that I am in this scene. But I need you to understand that I am not in this scene, you stunning snickerdoodle.

MIDI. And I need you to understand that... (*Shift.*) some things are entirely out of our control.

        (*Something changes.*)

DOLAN. I am completely in control of my feelings. And so are you, Riborg.

MIDI. *(As Riborg.)* I wish things were different—

DOLAN. If you truly loved me, you wouldn't marry him.

MIDI. *(As Riborg.)* I have no choice. This has been decided since before I was born—

DOLAN. It's your life, of course you have a choice!

MIDI. *(As Riborg.)* You have no idea what it is like to be a daughter, to be a woman—

DOLAN. Oh, yes, Riborg, tell me how awful it must be to be a rich and beautiful swan and have everything you ever wanted. Try being a poor and ugly orphan who has to make the world for themselves.

MIDI. *(As Riborg.)* Hans. You want to be a swan so desperately, that you don't understand—

DOLAN. THUNDER!

> *(Thunder. Lightning. Darkness.)*
>
> *(Lights up on **DOLAN**, alone.)*
>
> *(Except that **BESSIE** is creeping in behind him.)*
>
> *(Covered in a cloak? A poncho? Seemingly nefarious.)*

(To the heavens?) NO MORE BIZONKERDOODLE INTERRUPTIONS!!!

Especially because this next scene is my favorite scene from *The Little Mer*—I MEAN THE LITTLE RAIN CLOUD!!!!!!!!!!

SO!! Rain Cloud goes back to Ralmond and—

BESSIE. Mooooooo...

DOLAN. Oh no.
So I forgot to tell you: I've replaced you in the story.
Don't take it too personally.
It's not about you, it's all about me.

BESSIE. *(As Sea Witch.)* I know what you want, my pretty. You want to be human.

DOLAN. But…I am human?

BESSIE. *(As Sea Witch.)* How very foolish of you. It can only end in sorrow. I will make you a potion that will give you the prettiest pair of human legs you've ever seen.

DOLAN. All right, come on you heifer, your scene is done—

DOLAN. *(Trying to shoo* **BESSIE**.*)* Off you go!	**BESSIE**. *(As Sea Witch.)* But every time you walk, it will feel like walking on daggers. And I must be paid in kind. Your voice is very…powerful.
Move it, you belligerent bovine!	
	Give me your tongue and I will give you the potion.
Out or I'll turn you into jerky!	

(**BESSIE** *holds out…a glass of wine?)*

(**BESSIE** *does a dastardly, evil sea witch laugh, but it eventually morphs into laughing as a man.)*

DOLAN. What are you—Stop that!!! Stop laughing!

(Something changes.)

Stop laughing at me, Karl, you're being cruel!

BESSIE. *(As Karl.)* I'm sorry, Hans, but that is a truly ridiculous idea. Marrying Jenny Lind? She is the most lauded opera singer of our time.

DOLAN. But she loves me! She said so in her letters—I can show you—

BESSIE. *(As Karl.)* You really think she would choose *you* over the dozens of men who are seeking her hand.

DOLAN. She says my stories are exquisite and that she loves my company and—

> (**BESSIE** *chuckles.*)

Well, you've enjoyed my company in the past. Haven't you, Karl?

BESSIE. *(As Karl.)* ...May I remind you that I am a Grand Duke. And we are in public.

DOLAN. And may I remind you that I am the greatest writer of our time! You should be honored to be seen in public with *me*!

BESSIE. *(As Karl.)* Oh, Hans. You may have an invitation to high society, but don't ever let that fool you into forgetting who you truly are.

DOLAN. And who am I, Karl?

> (**BESSIE** *sighs and hands the glass to* **DOLAN**.*)*

BESSIE. *(As Karl...?)* Why don't you stay quiet for once, Mr. Hans Christian Andersen, and have a drink. Wine can really change your...perspective...

> (**DOLAN** *is about to take the glass and* **BESSIE** *stops him.)*

Ah-ah! That. For the drink.

> (**BESSIE** *gestures to the book.)*

> (**DOLAN**, *in a state of confusion, hands her the book and she hands him the glass of wine. He stares at the glass.)*

> (**BESSIE** *opens the book and reads.)*

Once upon a time...

DOLAN. *(Gasps, realizing what has happened.)* GIMME THAT BACK—!!!

THE DIFFERENT FEMALE VOICE & BESSIE. Deep in the sea, where the water is as blue as the prettiest cornflower—

DOLAN. *(To the ether.)* And YOU! WHO ARE YOU?!

> (**BESSIE** *rips the pages out as* **THE DIFFERENT FEMALE VOICE** *reads, dodging* **DOLAN** *who is trying to both find the* **VOICE** *and get his book back.)*

DOLAN. Stop it!! That's not the story I'm telling!

WHERE ARE YOU COMING FROM?!

(To **BESSIE**.*)* What are you doing?? STOP THAT!! NO!!

This is not what I had planned at all—why is no one doing what they are supposed to be doing—why doesn't anyone want me to tell my happy story with a happy ending that has nothing to do with my personal life.

I'm just trying to tell *The Little Rain Cloud*!!!!

THE DIFFERENT FEMALE VOICE. The youngest mermaid was the prettiest of them all; beautiful and delicate as a rose-leaf—

Within the flower, sat a very delicate and graceful little maiden—

When the queen saw how beautiful and sweet she was, she grew spiteful—

The little duckling had been so belittled for his ugliness—

The Nightingale! Thumbelina! The Little Match Girl! The Ugly Duckling! The Little Mermaid!

> (**DOLAN** *finally gets his hands on the book and yanks it from* **BESSIE**.*)*

DOLAN. YOU ARE MY CHARACTERS AND I CONTROL YOU.

BESSIE. You think you can control us just because you wrote us?

BESSIE & THE DIFFERENT FEMALE VOICE. You're so silly, Uncle Hans.

DOLAN. What?!

> *(Thunder. Lightning.)*
>
> *(A child crying can be heard from somewhere.)*
>
> *(**BESSIE** snatches the book back and runs away mooing, ripping out more pages.)*

NO!! WAIT! WAIT!

> *(**DOLAN** tries to chase after **BESSIE** but **INA** enters, looking a little different.)*

INA. *(As Jette.)* Hans?

> *(**DOLAN** freezes. He is so paralyzed he cannot speak to her.)*
>
> *(**RALMOND** runs onstage, out of breath, arms outstretched.)*

RALMOND. I love the rain!

INA. *(As Jette.)* He proposed! He proposed to me! What do I do?

RALMOND. I love the rain!

INA. *(As Jette.)* I know, I know, he's an idiot... But I think I... I think I love him.

RALMOND. I love the rain!

INA. *(As Jette.)* You're right. Thank you. Oh, Hans, I'm getting married.

(**INA** *hugs* **DOLAN** *and then exits.*)

(**DOLAN** *clutches his body and is visibly distraught.*)

(**RAIN CLOUD** *appears, looking at a* **LITTLE GIRL** *crying.*)

(**RALMOND** *spots* **RAIN CLOUD**.)

RALMOND. There you are! What are you doing over there?

RAIN CLOUD. This small human is raining from her face. And I thought maybe she was a rain cloud who had managed to become human.

RALMOND. She's just…crying. That's the human rain. It waters our hearts. Your rain waters the Earth.

RAIN CLOUD. Bessie says I'm hurting the Earth with this flooding. Is that true, Ralmond?

RALMOND. Yes…but you're doing it for me, aren't you? Because you love me?

RAIN CLOUD. Yes…or…at least I think I do…

One: You hate umbrellas—

RALMOND. One: You hate umbrellas, too.

RAIN CLOUD. Two: You enjoy the rain—

RALMOND. Two: You are the rain.

RAIN CLOUD. Three: You see me…

RALMOND. Three: *You* see me.

RAIN CLOUD. One and two and three… you were made for me.

RALMOND. Right.

One and two and three.

We are meant to be.

RAIN CLOUD. We…are…?

(**RALMOND** *nods and moves closer.*)

(*He slowly touches* **RAIN CLOUD**'s *cheek. It is air. His fingers tingle.*)

(*He leans in slowly for a kiss.*)

(*At first, it's weird. Because he's kissing the air.*)

(*But then.* **RALMOND** *and* **RAIN CLOUD** *really kiss.*)

(*At that same moment,* **DOLAN** *drinks the wine.*)

(*Then he immediately tries to cough it back out.*)

DOLAN. Aww nutbuggins.

(*Thunder. Lightning.*)

(*Lots and lots of it.*)

(*Mixed in is a siren song and some moos.**)

(*The thunder pulls* **RALMOND** *and* **RAIN CLOUD** *apart from each other.*)

(**DOLAN**, **RALMOND**, *and* **RAIN CLOUD** *are suspended in time.*)

(*The three of them take a big gasp of air.*)

(*And then they all begin to undergo a good ol' magical, fairy tale transformation—complete with music and sparkles!**)

(**RALMOND** *is becoming air.*)

(**RAIN CLOUD** *is becoming human.*)

(And **DOLAN** *is...also becoming a human? But a mermaid-turned-human.)*

(When their transformations are complete, **RALMOND** *collapses to the floor unconscious,* **DOLAN** *collapses to the floor because he finds his legs are in pain, and* **RAIN CLOUD** *manages to land on her feet, though a little unbalanced from the new feeling of weight and gravity.)*

(Then **RAIN CLOUD** *notices* **RALMOND** *unconscious on the stage covered in flood/ book pages.)*

(It has stopped raining.)

RAIN CLOUD. Oh. Fuck.

*(***RAIN CLOUD** *rushes to him.)*

Oh no. Oh nononononono. Please be alive! Please be alive!

*(***RAIN CLOUD** *listens for breath.)*

*(***EDVARD** *runs onstage, he picks* **DOLAN** *up.)*

*(***DOLAN** *squirms to get out.)*

EDVARD. I got you, I got you! Woah there—I'm just trying to help you!

*(***DOLAN** *sees* **EDVARD***'s face. He stares. Then he tries to speak to him but no sound comes out of his mouth. He realizes this and grabs his throat.)*

It's okay—you're okay! I'll take you to my castle—We'll help you!

*(***EDVARD** *exits carrying* **DOLAN***.)*

RAIN CLOUD. I feel like you're not breathing, are you breathing? Am I breathing? I'm breathing... oh. Weird. Hold on. I'll um.

> (**RAIN CLOUD** *lifts up his body and almost trips when she realizes how light he is.*)

Wow. You're as light as a... light as a cloud! *(Laughs.)* Oh, I get it now. It is a funny joke, Ralmond, because you're a rain— *(Gasps.)* OH NO!

> (**RAIN CLOUD** *exits carrying* **RALMOND**.*)
>
> (*An empty stage.*)
>
> (*Except the* **LITTLE GIRL** *from before, who begins to cry again.*)
>
> (*She is the* **LITTLE ONE** *and the owner of* **THE DIFFERENT FEMALE VOICE**.*)
>
> (*We hear the sound of the deep sea.*)
>
> (*Growing.*)
>
> (*And growing.*)
>
> (**MIDI** *appears in the apartment, making a call.*)
>
> (*She is quietly whispering, "Please pick up, please pick up."*)
>
> (*Voicemail.*)

MIDI. Hi, it's me again—just—please, please call me back when you get this—the news says the power is out in half the city—I just want to know you're okay.

> (*She throws the phone down.*)
>
> (*She sees pages on the floor.*)
>
> (*She picks them up—where did they come from?*)

(She sees The Little Mermaid *book on the table.)*

(She opens it, looking for where the pages go.)

(She starts reading aloud.)

MIDI. "Her sisters noticed that their youngest had not left her room or tended to her garden. They approached her to find tears streaming down her face. 'Why are you crying?' they asked."

LITTLE ONE. I don't know. I've never felt like this before. I feel so awful. And yet so happy.

MIDI. "You have been acting so strangely since you went up Above."

LITTLE ONE. I saw the most wonderful things. Fish in the sky, and hot, red, flowers dancing on a shore. But I also saw...a human. And I cannot stop thinking of him. I want to be with him. I want to be him. I want him. What is this?

MIDI. "Perhaps it is love."

LITTLE ONE. What is love?

MIDI. "We're not quite sure what love is. But we can offer you a dictionary definition. Love is a formula for ending an affectionate letter, as in 'Take care. Love, Bessie.'" ...That's weird... What translation is this? Umm... "The Little Mermaid sighed and said,"

MIDI & LITTLE ONE. "I would gladly give all the hundreds of years that I have to live, to be a human being only for one day, and to have the hope of knowing the happiness of that world above."

> *(At some point,* **LITTLE ONE** *went over to* **MIDI***'s apartment and began reading the line over her shoulder.)*

LITTLE ONE. May I see that?

*(**MIDI**, stunned, says nothing, sticks the pages in the book and hands it over.)*

Thank you.

*(**LITTLE ONE** skips off, reading the book.)*

MIDI. Oh my god I'm going insane. It's this rain. It's all the rain's fault.

*(**RAIN CLOUD** bursts through the door, carrying **RALMOND**.)*

RAIN CLOUD. Hi Midi!

MIDI. Ralmond!! Come in, please! Here, let me help you.

*(**RAIN CLOUD** sets him gently on the couch.)*

What happened to him? I feel like he's not breathing— is he? The rain is ruining everything.

RAIN CLOUD. Hey now.

MIDI. Oh my god, oh my god, is he all right?

RAIN CLOUD. I think he's okay, but, Midi, you should know—

MIDI. I'm sorry, do I know you?

RAIN CLOUD. ...Not exactly—

MIDI. How do you know my name? Who are you?

RAIN CLOUD. I'm not 100% sure how to answer that question, but I could tell you who I *was*! Or *what* I was...which was...a rain cloud? With a soul?

*(Pause. **MIDI** puts her face in her hands. She breathes loudly.)*

MIDI. Go on.

RAIN CLOUD. Are you sure?

MIDI. GO.

RAIN CLOUD. Okay! Uh, I was a rain cloud, and I fell in love with Ralmond, and I wanted to become human so he could love me back and so I tried to woo him—sorry—but Ralmond kept rejecting me so no worries—and then for some reason Ralmond found me. And then. Something happened. And then—

MIDI. What "something" happened?

RAIN CLOUD. Oh that's really not important right now, but after that, maybe I struck lightning or something because all this energy burst out of nowhere and Ralmond and I...I think we switched. Like not switched bodies, because clearly I don't look like him, but switched places in the world? Because now I'm a human and he's a...rain cloud.

MIDI. Ask me what I had for breakfast this morning.

RAIN CLOUD. What did you have for breakfast this morning?

MIDI. Two hard-boiled eggs and a coffee with Splenda. I can't remember my breakfast in dreams. So...this... this is real... But Ralmond is still...alive?

RAIN CLOUD. He still...exists?

MIDI. What caused this in the first place? Can you do the opposite of that?

RAIN CLOUD. What would be the opposite of a k—uhh!! You know, by the way, you should add a fruit, like a grapefruit to your first meal of the day. *(Gasp.)* I know what a grapefruit is!

MIDI. ...Rallie eats grapefruits in the morning...

(**RAIN CLOUD** *points to objects in the room.*)

RAIN CLOUD. Chair. Couch. Clock. Invisible wifi. This is crazy! Lamp. Carpet stain. And I knew you were Midi. And I knew how to get to your apartment. I must have gotten Rallie's knowledge!

MIDI. Don't call him that. Only I call him that.

RAIN CLOUD. You look stressed, Midi. Stressed. That's a negative emotion when one is overwhelmed with thoughts or feelings. Oh!

> (**RAIN CLOUD** *tries to put her forehead on* **MIDI***'s.* **MIDI** *pushes her back so* **RAIN CLOUD** *lands near the leak.*)

MIDI. What are you doing?!

RAIN CLOUD. You touch foreheads when you're stressed!

MIDI. Only Rallie and I do that. That's our thing. You don't get to do that.

> (**RAIN CLOUD** *feels a drop from the leak in the apartment.*)

RAIN CLOUD. Oh, and that's a drop of water! Haha, a *rain* drop.

> (*Drip.*)

And this is how water feels.

> (*Drip.*)

And this is...how...water feels...

> (*Drip.*)

This is how water feels!! THIS IS HOW WATER FEELS, MIDI!!

MIDI. Okay, little rain human person. This is not cute. What do I do, right now? How do I fix this?

RAIN CLOUD. I do not know. And when I do not know something I go ask...the internet! Wait. That doesn't sound right... Who do I ask...?

MIDI. This little act may have worked on Ralmond but it's not working on me. So what can I give you or do for you to tell me how to fix this? Money? Food? What do you want?

RAIN CLOUD. I want you. I love you.

MIDI. What?

RAIN CLOUD. What.

MIDI. Did you just say—?!

RAIN CLOUD. I said I want you...r bathroom. To go there. To use it. To...pee? Huh, that's a kind of human rain too.

MIDI. Um, okay... the bathroom is over—

> (**MIDI** *goes to show her where it is but notices* **RALMOND** *is gone.*)

> (*At some point during the above, he evaporated.*)

Oh my god where is he? He was just here—he couldn't have just—oh god. Rallie? Rallie?!

> (**MIDI** *looks around.* **RAIN CLOUD** *goes to the window and tries to look up.*)

RAIN CLOUD. I think he went back. To the sky.

MIDI. No he's not going *back*. He's from here. This Earth. As a living, breathing, human being.

RAIN CLOUD. But, like I told you, when he kissed me there was a weird switching of energies and—

MIDI. ...He kissed you? And that's what... you're telling me that's when all this...?

> (*Thunder. Lightning.*)

> (**MIDI** *yelps.*)

> (*Suddenly, it starts to pour.*)

RAIN CLOUD. That...might be him.

> (**MIDI** *looks out at the rain. She tries to shake all this weirdness off.*)

MIDI. I have to find Ralmond before he drowns or something worse. You—you stay here. I'll figure out, how to, um, get you to a professional later.

(**MIDI** *runs out.*)

RAIN CLOUD. Wait, Midi! You won't be able to find Ralmond on—

(**RAIN CLOUD** *sees on a shoe on her way out.*)

A shoelace! A shoelace... Hmm. I still don't get it!

(*A distant moo.*)

Bessie! Oh no, I promised I wouldn't forget her! She needs grass!

(**RAIN CLOUD** *runs out the door.*)

(**BESSIE** *swims across the stage.*)

BESSIE. Moo! [Translation: Must find Rain Cloud. Must find grass.]

Moo! [Translation: Follow the...thunder.]

(*Thunder. Lightning.*)

(**LITTLE ONE** *enters reading aloud from the book.*)

LITTLE ONE. The Prince brought the Little Mermaid to his castle and tried to help her heal.

(**EDVARD** *carries on* **DOLAN** *and sets him on a bed.*)

(**DOLAN**, *once let go, immediately tries to bolt, but he falls from the pain in his feet.* **EDVARD** *helps him back up.*)

EDVARD. Did you hurt your legs? I'll call the doctor for you. What's your name?

(**DOLAN** *is staring at* **EDVARD**'s *face, still shocked.*)

LITTLE ONE. Without her voice, all she could do was stare back at him.

EDVARD. You can't speak? Oh no, I'm sorry...

LITTLE ONE. Every step she took she felt as if treading upon sharp knives; but she bore it willingly, for every moment beside the Prince was a moment of bliss.

EDVARD. My home is yours. We'll take good care of you here.

LITTLE ONE. Her love for this human world and the Prince only grew stronger. And his affection for her grew stronger too.

EDVARD. It's so strange... I feel like I know you. Like I can tell you anything.

LITTLE ONE. But alas, the Prince had a deep longing for someone he could not have as well. The mysterious young maiden who he believed saved his life.

EDVARD. When I'm with you, I almost forget about her.

LITTLE ONE. And what's more, he was engaged to a princess from another kingdom.

EDVARD. I hope you never feel this horrible pang of loving someone you can never be with.

(**DOLAN** *facepalms.*)

LITTLE ONE. Then the fated day came when the Prince was to meet his betrothed.

EDVARD. I can't marry someone I've never met! I can't spend a life with someone I do not love. I'd much rather marry...you.

(**DOLAN** *is like, "wait, are you serious?"*)

LITTLE ONE. Translation: Wait, are you serious?

EDVARD. Wow, I'm going insane. Sorry. Why would you ever want to marry an idiot like me?

(**DOLAN** *faceplants in the bed.*)

LITTLE ONE. Translation: The biggest idiot alive.

EDVARD. Well. Here I go. Wish me luck.

LITTLE ONE. Translation: Good luck, you opulent oaf.

(**DOLAN** *gives a look to the* **LITTLE ONE** *like, "Hey! Why do you have access to my inner monologues?"*)

(**EDVARD** *leaves* **DOLAN** *to be introduced to a* **PRINCESS** *underneath a veil.*)

The Prince was prepared to call off the arranged marriage. But of all miraculous occurrences, the Prince was betrothed to his one true love.

(**INA** *removes her veil.* **EDVARD** *faints.*)

INA. Oh dear lord.

(**INA** *moves over to him. He awakes and grabs her.*)

EDVARD. Ina, I need you to know I didn't fall in love with you at first sight! I fell in love with you when you asked me the second time which way the seamstress was and stomped on my foot! I felt like that was the first time anyone had ever seen me as just a person I need you to know that—I NEED YOU TO KNOW THAT—

INA. SHUT!!! UP!!!!!

EDVARD. SORRY!!!

INA. YOU CAN'T HAVE FALLEN IN LOVE WITH ME BECAUSE OF THE SEAMSTRESS BECAUSE I FELL IN LOVE WITH YOU BECAUSE OF THE SEAMSTRESS.

EDVARD. ...What?!

INA. I knew you were the Prince I was engaged to, and I went and found you in your village so I could prove you were an idiot and demand my father call off the whole arrangement and you were an idiot but an idiot who knew which way the local seamstress was and I couldn't stop thinking about that LIKE A DUMMY!!

EDVARD. Ohmygodohmygodohmygodohmygod—

(**INA** *screams in his face and then runs away.*)

Ina! Wait! Wife! THIS IS THE BEST DAY OF MY LIFE.

(**EDVARD** *chases after her.*)

LITTLE ONE. The Little Mermaid's heart sank. Any chance the Prince would choose to marry her had washed away. How she longed to tell him that she was the one, the one who saved his life, the one he was meant to be with. But the Prince would never know...

And there was Thunder!! Lightning!! Crash!! Boom!!!

(*Thunder. Lighting. Crash. Boom.*)

(*It is raining.*)

(**MIDI** *and* **RAIN CLOUD** *running through the water.*)

(**MIDI** *with an umbrella.*)

MIDI. I told you to stay home—it's dangerous out here!

RAIN CLOUD. I need to find my cowfriend, Bessie!

MIDI. There are no cows in this city!

RAIN CLOUD. But I can hear her somewhere near. Moooo! Mooo!! Bessie!! Could Ralmond speak cow? I don't think I can speak cow anymore!

MIDI. Actually he spoke antelope—

> (**RAIN CLOUD** *collapses.*)

Are you okay?

RAIN CLOUD. I'm… I'm…exhausted.

MIDI. Yeah, 'cause you've been sprinting this whole way.

RAIN CLOUD. I used to cross cities within a few seconds!

MIDI. Well, humans don't do that.

RAIN CLOUD. This feels terrible. Ugh. Human bodies… are so…limiting…

MIDI. Here let me help you up.

> (**MIDI** *puts out her hand.* **RAIN CLOUD** *grabs it and gets up. This is her first real human touch. She stumbles because it freaks her out and* **MIDI** *catches her.* **RAIN CLOUD** *stares at* **MIDI**.)

Are you sure you're okay?

RAIN CLOUD. …

MIDI. Hey? Do you want to rest?

RAIN CLOUD. Um, maybe. Maybe that will be good. Rest is good. Rest is good, right?

MIDI. Yeah.

> (*They find a place to sit.* **RAIN CLOUD** *decidedly sits with distance in between her and* **MIDI**. *They sit for a bit. Lol that rhymes.*)

*(Knock at the door in **DOLAN**'s world.)*

*(**INA** pokes her head in.)*

*(**LITTLE ONE**, reading from the book, speaks **DOLAN**'s thoughts amidst his gestures.)*

INA. It's just me.

LITTLE ONE. Translation: Oh my god, how do I look?

INA. May I come in?

LITTLE ONE. Translation: I'd rather you didn't but you're royalty so…

INA. I brought you a little something. A little accessory from my country. I thought maybe you could wear it to the wedding?

LITTLE ONE. Translation: It's not really my color…

INA. I could help put it on—

> *(**DOLAN** shies away from her touch and puts it on himself.)*

It looks so good on you.

LITTLE ONE. Translation: …Thank you… I mean, obviously, I look good in anything.

INA. *(Gestures to the seat next to him.)* May I?

> *(**DOLAN** nods.)*

> *(**INA** sits next to him. They also sit for a bit.)*

MIDI. Do you want to come under the umbrella?

RAIN CLOUD. I hate umbrellas. Blegh.

MIDI. Rallie hates umbrellas too.

RAIN CLOUD. I know! That's why I thought we were meant to be.

MIDI. Maybe you are... He loves the rain and I do not.

RAIN CLOUD. Because you're scared of thunder and lightning?

MIDI. How did you—?

RAIN CLOUD. Sorry, all of Ralmond's knowledge is just *(Points to her brain.)* up in here so I know a lot about you. *(Remembering something maybe a little too intimate.)* Maybe, um, maybe too much...about you...

MIDI. But I never told him that. I've never told anyone that.

RAIN CLOUD. Well, he knew. That's why he waits for you to fall asleep first on stormy nights. Why haven't you told anyone?

MIDI. It's just so...embarrassing... I'm a grown woman afraid of thunder and lightning... like, I know there's an infinitesimally small chance of getting struck but still... And I don't like the rain because it reminds me of this irrational fear. I hate things that are irrational or uncontrollable...

RAIN CLOUD. Like love?

MIDI. *(Laughs a little.)* ...It's funny, love comes so easy for Ralmond—he's always been a dreamer, a romantic. The exact opposite of me... I mean, we truly don't make any sense together, we make as much a sense as a—

RAIN CLOUD. As a shoelace?

MIDI. ...What?

RAIN CLOUD. Oh, uh, Ralmond once said he loves you because a shoelace. But it's funny, even with everything I know about you now, I still have no idea what that means. Do you?

MIDI. ...No...

RAIN CLOUD. ...Then...why are you crying?

MIDI. I don't know... I just... I suddenly really missed him.

RAIN CLOUD. Oh...it's okay, Midi. Crying is good. Crying waters our hearts.

> (**RAIN CLOUD** *reaches over cautiously and catches a tear from* **MIDI***'s face with her finger.*)

Look at that. See, not all rain is bad.

> (**MIDI** *laughs. For a moment,* **RAIN CLOUD** *feels drawn into her but then stops herself.*)

MIDI. Well, maybe if Rallie's really a rain cloud, I guess I... I love the rain.

> (*Thunder, lightning, a gasp.*)

> (*It stops raining.*)

> (**RALMOND** *falls into* **MIDI***'s arms.*)

OH MY GOD WHAT IS HAPPENING?

RALMOND. Oh my god what is happening?

RAIN CLOUD. Ralmond!

MIDI. Ralmond?

RALMOND. Ralmond?

MIDI. Oh god, oh god, what happ—are you okay?

RALMOND. Oh god, oh god, what happ—are you okay?

MIDI. I'm fine, but you—?!

RALMOND. I'm fine, but you...?

MIDI. Me?

RALMOND. Me? ...I love you.

RAIN CLOUD. This is exactly what happened to me!

MIDI. What do I do now??

RAIN CLOUD. Bessie will know! She's out here somewhere, we gotta find her.

(**RAIN CLOUD** *runs off, maybe mooing.*)

MIDI. Wait! Rain Cloud!

RALMOND. I love you!

MIDI. Oh god, you're as light as a cloud!

RALMOND. I am a cloud.

MIDI. No, you're not!

(**MIDI** *chases after* **RAIN CLOUD** *with* **RALMOND** *in her arms.*)

(*Back to* **INA** *and* **DOLAN**:)

INA. The sea is beautiful today.

LITTLE ONE. Translation: It looks the same as always.

INA. My kingdom is surrounded by mountains, so the water is very new for me.

LITTLE ONE. Translation: I hate the mountains. They're just giant land wrinkles.

INA. Do you like it here?

LITTLE ONE. Translation: ...Me?

INA. I hear you're also not from around here.

LITTLE ONE. Translation: Oh...um, it's okay.

INA. Perhaps it's hard to look around when a particular someone has all of your attention.

LITTLE ONE. Translation: Um, what? Um. I don't know who you're talking about.

INA. (*Small laugh.*) I don't blame you. The Prince has his ways of being—

LITTLE ONE. Translation: Idiotic. Insane. Ignorant.

INA. Frustratingly forgivable.

> (**DOLAN** *looks at* **INA.**)

I know. It's not fair. We work so hard to be so sensible and strong and careful. And then someone like him comes along and all that effort...dissolves. I've been trying to figure out what it is about him, what he has over every other human that exists. But I've... I've given up. He just...he just...is. And I am... I am so... I...

> (**DOLAN** *hands her a pillow.*)
>
> (*He gestures like, "Scream into the pillow, hun."*)
>
> (*She does.*)

LITTLE ONE. You mustn't feel shame or guilt about being in love.

INA. Isn't true love supposed to be much harder to find?

LITTLE ONE. Sometimes. But...sometimes not. That's just the way the world works.

> (**DOLAN** *looks at* **LITTLE ONE**. **LITTLE ONE** *nods at* **DOLAN**.)
>
> (*Something changes, but a little differently this time.*)

INA. (*As Jette.*) Thank you, Hans. You are so dear to me. To Edvard too! I hope you understand that.

LITTLE ONE. Don't lie to me, Jette.

INA. (*As Jette.*) It's the truth! Once, while you were ill, Edvard was so worried that he walked right into me. I completely disappeared from his vision.

LITTLE ONE. Well then you're about to marry the biggest fool to walk the planet because everyone who does not spend every moment of their time looking at you is wasting their life away. WASTING!!

INA. *(As Jette.)* You're so dramatic, Hans.

LITTLE ONE. Who me? Dramatic?

> (**INA** *laughs.*)

When he drives you mad, you come running to me, and I will teach you how to handle his temper tantrums— and never expect him to handle spiders, he's terrible with spiders.

INA. *(As Jette.)* And when he tires of me, you can teach him how to handle *my* temper tantrums.

LITTLE ONE. Except he has no good excuse to ever tire of you, Jette.

> (**INA** *kisses* **DOLAN**'s *hand.*)

INA. *(As Jette...?)* I will see you at the wedding, yes? It will make us both so happy to see you there.

LITTLE ONE. I wouldn't miss it for the world.

INA. Goodnight, Little One. Dream sweetly.

> (**INA** *exits.*)

LITTLE ONE. The Little Mermaid watched forlornly as the bride and bridegroom wed. Her heart broke for the Prince. But it also broke because this would be the last day she would be human, for tomorrow, she would dissolve into seafoam—

> (**DOLAN** *barrels through the pain, sneaks over to* **LITTLE ONE** *and puts his hands on the book.*)

DOLAN.   Gotcha!

LITTLE ONE. No, I'm telling the story, Uncle Hans!

> (**LITTLE ONE** *yanks the book and runs away.* **DOLAN** *chases after her.*)

(**BESSIE** *runs across the stage.*)

BESSIE. MOO! [Translation: CHASE SEQUENCE!]

(*A chase sequence!*)

(*The* **CHARACTERS** *each individually run across the stage as they cry out their line.*)

RAIN CLOUD. (*Chasing after* **BESSIE.**) Wait! BESSIE! Wait!

MIDI. (*Chasing after* **RAIN CLOUD.**) Wait! Rain Cloud! Wait!

RALMOND. (*Chasing after* **MIDI.**) Wait! Midi! Wait!

INA. (*Running away.*) Wait! No! Wait!

EDVARD. (*Chasing after* **INA.**) Wait! Ina! Wait!

LITTLE ONE. (*Running away.*) You can't catch me!

(**DOLAN** *grunts as he is seen trying to run after* **LITTLE ONE.**)

(*Everyone then starts to yell at once, chasing each other around the stage.*)

(*Chaos.*)

(*Eventually,* **DOLAN** *catches up to* **LITTLE ONE** *and grabs the book.*)

(*They tug of war on the book.*)

DOLAN. Give! Me! Back! My! Stories!

(*The book flies out of both of their hands and out fall pages from the book, except they look more like letters now.*)

Wait, those are my—

(*As he scrambles to pick them up from the floor, the* **REST OF THE CAST** *each picks up a letter and reads:*)

RALMOND. Dearest Harald Scharff—

RAIN CLOUD. My dear Louise Collin—

MIDI. To the lovely Riborg Voigt—

BESSIE. To the Grand Duke of Weimar, Karl Alexander August Johann—

INA. Henriette "Jette" Thyberg, delight of my life—

EDVARD. Dear...Edvard...

> (**LITTLE ONE** *picks the book back up and runs off.*)

My soul is sick, in love with you.

EDVARD, RAIN CLOUD & INA. You invade my every thought.

ALL EXCEPT DOLAN & LITTLE ONE. You have even entered my stories.

> (*At this point, the* **CAST**, *minus* **DOLAN** *and* **LITTLE ONE**, *should find a section of the audience to say something like the following:*)

"Hi! I'm supposed to tell you who [name of Hans Christian Andersen's lovefriend they play] was and how they showed up in Hans Christian Andersen's stories—but honestly, that sounds kind of boring. So I'm going to tell you a love story of my own instead."

> (*And then proceed to tell the audience their own love story. Only as personal and as revealing as the actor is comfortable with it being. Their first crush, their first kiss, their first dog [this one goes over very well], how they met their best friend. Whatever they like.*)

> (*Meanwhile* **DOLAN**, *who is most certainly* **HANS**, *is still picking up his letters and perhaps he even proceeds to read them, getting lost in his own past feelings of desire.*)

(And once the stories start to wrap up, **EDVARD** *starts calling out* **HANS**' *name.)*

EDVARD. HANS! Do you hear yourself?? Your letters are inappropriate—

HANS. My letters are gifts! Every ounce as poetic as my stories—

EDVARD. You cannot confess your love to every human who shows you kindness—

HANS. What do you care? Who I fall in love with has nothing to do with you—

EDVARD. Everything you do affects me, affects Jette— You have been part of this family since my father took you in—

HANS. Family?! Does family get uninvited from each other's homes? From the most important day of their life—

EDVARD. After cleaning up every single social mess you get into, I deserved a break—

HANS. And *I* deserved to be at your wedding!

EDVARD. ...You know exactly why I couldn't have you at my wedding.

(A deep silence between them.)

HANS. No. NO. You don't—You don't get to say that unless you feel the gut-wrenching pain and torture that I suffer through every time you—

*(**LITTLE ONE** bursts in with the book in her hand.)*

LITTLE ONE. FATHER!! How DARE you keep Uncle Hans from me??!!

EDVARD. What are you doing out of bed—

LITTLE ONE. Uncle Hans, I finished my version of *The Little Mermaid*! May I show you? I think I've made it more brilliant and dramatic than the original!

HANS. Excuse me—?!

LITTLE ONE. So when we left off, the Prince and Princess confess their love for each other—

HANS. You are still giving too much attention to those two idiots!

LITTLE ONE. But Uncle Hans! They are most romantic love story you ever told! They are the real deal!

(**HANS** *looks at* **EDVARD.**)

So then the Little Mermaid is sad because she's going to become seafoam, but then her sisters show up and they say to her:

> "Sister, we have sacrificed our hair to the Sea Witch in exchange for this dagger. Cut the Prince's heart out, and you can rejoin us as a sister of the sea."

And then the Little Mermaid points the dagger at the Prince—but then she realizes—she can't kill him! Because she loves him! And! That will make his new wife so sad! And AND! She doesn't want to go back to being a mermaid! She hated it! "But, wait a minute!" She thinks! "Seafoam? I've never been seafoam before! That sounds kinda fun, why not give it a try!" So then she stands on the deck of the ship and—!

(**EDVARD** *scoops her up in a giant hug.*)

EDVARD. That sounds incredible, my little genius storyteller. And I am so looking forward to hearing the rest of it tomorrow.

LITTLE ONE. But I need to show Uncle Hans and he never visits anymore—

EDVARD. Uncle Hans will come back next week.

HANS. I will?

LITTLE ONE. Oh, good! I'm so looking forward to seeing my colleague again! Next time I will show you my adaptation of *The Snow Queen*!

HANS. Why is everyone obsessed with that one?

LITTLE ONE. Goodnight, Uncle Hans! May I give you a kiss?

(*He kneels for her. She pecks him on the cheek.*)

HANS. Now tell your father he must do the same when he goes to bed.

LITTLE ONE. Father, Uncle Hans says you must—

EDVARD. I heard him, thank you, Little One.

HANS. Goodnight, sweet pea. Ooh. I should write a story about a princess and a pea.

LITTLE ONE. Can't wait! Goodnight, Father.

(**LITTLE ONE** *hugs* **EDVARD** *before running off.*)

HANS. Why can't I have what she has?

(**EDVARD** *looks at* **HANS**. *He opens his mouth to say something when:*)

Why can't someone love and see and hold me and only me for the rest of my life?

EDVARD. Hans... Love is so much more—

HANS. (*Mockingly.*) *So much more complicated than that!* So much more complicated than poor, ugly, stupid, orphan Hans will ever understand.

EDVARD. I wish you wouldn't do that.

HANS. Do what?

EDVARD. You write this cruel narrative about yourself where you are perpetually a victim—

HANS. All I can do is write narratives! That is how I survive this vicious world. And I don't know if you've heard, but I'm quite good at it—I'm the greatest storyteller in DECADES!

EDVARD. No, in centuries!

HANS. No, in CENTU—oh, I mean, YES! That's right!

EDVARD. Although, you may have a rival. My Little One has quite the knack for it.

HANS. Her? She's just retelling my stories—and incorrectly, by the way! The Little Mermaid doesn't *want* to become seafoam at the end, she chooses seafoam because she is willing to sacrifice her whole existence so that the Prince can be happy. Because that is what real love looks like, Edvard.

EDVARD. But he never asked for that, Hans! Have you ever thought about what he...! *(Sighs.)* I think it would be nice if she... if the Mermaid lives in a world where being seafoam is fun. Because then she makes the choice out of love for him *and* out of...love for herself... Maybe something you should consider... For a future edition, I mean.

HANS. Edvard Collin. Are you, a simple plebian, suggesting that I, genius writer, change the ending to my masterpiece? And people call ME self-aggrandizing— Have you taken a good look at yourself in the mirror lately and—

(**EDVARD** *kisses* **HANS** *on the cheek.)*

EDVARD. Goodnight, Mr. Duckling. Sleep well.

HANS. You forgot the "ugly" part.

EDVARD. I didn't. And you know that.

(**EDVARD** *exits.*)

HANS. Why must you always end me like that?

(The return of the weird laugh, but it is perhaps slower and more defeated.)

Well, Ladies and Gentlemen.

It's all true.

I am Hans Christian Andersen.

Surprise!

I guess I...wanted to tell you the story of *The Little Rain Cloud*

And give it a nice happy ending.

Unlike *The Little Mermaid.*

But the tragedy of my life must pervade all my stories.

Because I die alone.

Partner-less, family-less, childless...love-less...

(**BESSIE** *enters nonchalantly.*)

Ugh. Of course, I'm stuck with the cow.

Just you and me, Bessie.

Sidekicks in our own stories.

BESSIE. Fuck you. I'm not a sidekick in my own story. Just in this one.

HANS. But I thought...?

BESSIE. I have my own life outside of your imagination, dude. And my life? Is fucking great. I have seven lovers, eight children, only two of which are assholes, and I wasn't born in a slaughterhouse, which makes me a pretty privileged cow. Also my best friend is literally running around an unfamiliar city trying to find me. Rain Cloud loves me. And I love them.

HANS. Oh! Is this a romantic plot twist?

BESSIE. No, you fucker—Best friends love each other like nobody's business, okay? Now can you move out of the way? I'm about to do my death scene. This is, like, my super big moment.

(**HANS** *steps out of the way.*)

Hello everyone.

I'm Bessie. Moo.

I'm going to tell you the story of my epic death.

> Once there was a man in the city. Let's call him Jenkins.
>
> Jenkins was thrown out of his apartment with just his rifle and beef jerky. Because he cheated on his wife. What a jerk...y.
>
> So he wandered the streets of the city.
>
> Slowly eating his beef jerky. Until eventually he ran out. And he grew hungry.
>
> So hungry.
>
> He was starving.
>
> He grew delirious.
>
> Then.
>
> He saw some beef jerky swimming in the flood.
>
> And a lone bullet strikes Bessie in the third stomach.

HANS. WHAT?!

BESSIE. A lone bullet strikes Bessie in the third stomach.

HANS. I heard you, I'm just shocked.

BESSIE. Yeah, THIS is the plot twist.

(**BESSIE** *clears her throat.*)

(*Then she has a wonderfully dramatic death scene and collapses to the floor.*)

(**RAIN CLOUD** *runs onstage.*)

RAIN CLOUD. BESSIE NO!!!

(**MIDI** *runs on with* **RALMOND** *not far behind.*)

MIDI. Is that your cowfriend?

RAIN CLOUD. Bessie, I'm so sorry! I got so single-minded about getting Ralmond, I wasn't thinking about anything else even though I promised not to forget you. You gave me so much advice and I gave you nothing.

BESSIE. (*To audience.*) I'm just gonna do the translations folks, you get it by now. (*To* **RAIN CLOUD**.) Friendship is not transactional, Rain Cloud. Plus, I love giving advice, I'm pretty fucking wise. Now could you turn this way? I want to die on my good side.

RAIN CLOUD. Oh no... oh no... please don't die...

(**RAIN CLOUD** *hugs* **BESSIE**.)

MIDI. So...anything in there about turning Ralmond back into a human, or...?

(**RAIN CLOUD** *starts audibly crying.*)

Oh... oh, crap I'm so sorry...

(**MIDI** *tries to touch* **RAIN CLOUD**.)

RAIN CLOUD. No, no, Midi don't touch me, I don't need to feel more feelings right now! What are all these feelings—I hate these feelings—Why do I have to feel all these feelings—!

(**RALMOND** *puts his forehead on* **RAIN CLOUD**.)

RALMOND. Deep breath in.

> (**RAIN CLOUD** *does.*)

And out.

> (**RAIN CLOUD** *does.*)

MIDI. Feelings are hard. But even the toughest ones are gifts—they're proof that you're alive. I'm sorry your friend is dying. That's very sad. It's one of many sad things that can happen in life.

RAIN CLOUD. But it's all my fault and she's all alone and—

MIDI. She's not alone. You're here. And we're here too. And all the other creatures she's touched—we'll all remember her. She's leaving life very loved. But make sure she knows that before she goes.

RAIN CLOUD. Bessie. I love you. Thank you for everything. You are so loved.

HANS. Okay, okay.

I get it.

You're all trying to tell me that I was loved.

And that I don't die alone...

I know...

But you know...

It would be nice

Every once in a while

To be seen.

Just me.

> (**LITTLE ONE** *bursts in again.*)

> (*Perhaps Jette [***INA***] and* **EDVARD** *are seen on the outskirts, watching them.*)

LITTLE ONE. UNCLE HANS!

HANS. You're supposed to be in bed!

LITTLE ONE. But mother said I could tell you my brilliant rewrite of your story's ending.

HANS. All right, what makes you think you're allowed to rewrite masterpieces—

> (**LITTLE ONE** *laughs and hugs* **HANS**.)

LITTLE ONE. I love you, Uncle Hans!

HANS. ...I love you too.

LITTLE ONE. So! The Little Mermaid decides to become seafoam, just at the same time as Rain Cloud is saying goodbye to Bessie—

HANS. Wait, what?

LITTLE ONE. Remember? My adaptation of *The Little Mermaid* also interweaves a brand new story called *The Little Rain Cloud*—

ALL EXCEPT LITTLE ONE. Ohhhhh...

LITTLE ONE. Uncle Hans, will you be the Little Mermaid, walking to the edge of the ship, ready to become seafoam?

HANS. ...Of course.

> (*He gets in character.*)

LITTLE ONE. Perfect! Now, meanwhile, Bessie takes her final breaths and says:

BESSIE. Thank you, Rain Cloud. I love you too. Before I go, I need to tell you some crucial plot information: You switched entities with Ralmond, so the only way he can become human again is if someone decides to become a rain cloud in his place.

RAIN CLOUD. I should go back to being a rain cloud, I'm too selfish to be a human.

BESSIE. Nah, that's just part of being human. And right now, you seem the most like yourself that I've ever seen you. All right, I gotta go. See ya around, Rain Cloud.

> *(**BESSIE** waves and dies. **RAIN CLOUD** waves back.)*

RALMOND. I can stay a rain cloud! And I can make it stop flooding! And then the Earth will be happy and Midi will be happy and Midi will love me—

MIDI. But I do love you, Rallie! So much. But we love differently. You love like water flows. And I love like grass grows. And maybe we can make that work or maybe we can't—I don't know! —But you can't sacrifice who you are for me. You love feeling the rain more than anything, and you can't do that if you *are* the rain. There just has to be another option...

> *(They are all like "Hmm...")*

> *(**HANS** walks over to **RAIN CLOUD**, **MIDI**, and **RALMOND**.)*

HANS. Um... Hi. Hello. Hi. Are you...looking for someone who wants to become a rain cloud? Because I would like to become seafoam and...well... seafoam and rain clouds... they are all part of the same water cycle, aren't they?

> *(Everyone looks to **BESSIE** wherever she is and she gives a thumbs up. Everyone cheers.)*

MIDI. Thank you so much!

LITTLE ONE. And with that, the Little Mermaid blows a kiss goodbye to the sleeping Prince and Princess.

> *(**HANS** blows a kiss to **EDVARD** and Jette [**INA**].)*

> And she jumps into the water!

(**HANS** *dives into the water.*)

(*Thunder. Lightning.*)

(**HANS** *disappears.*)

(**RALMOND** *takes a huge gasp of air and stumbles and* **MIDI** *steadies him.*)

(*They put their foreheads together.*)

MIDI. Hi.

RALMOND. Hi.

(**RALMOND** *and* **MIDI** *look to* **RAIN CLOUD.**)

RALMOND & MIDI. Hi.

(**RAIN CLOUD** *waves at them.*)

LITTLE ONE. And Midi and Ralmond have a very long, grown-up conversation that I am much too little to understand.

And Rain Cloud takes a job on a dairy farm

And makes sure all the cows live comfortably, with all the grass they need.

And she and Midi and Ralmond...

Whatever happens, they all stay close.

And as for the Little Mermaid...

(*The* **CAST** *makes the world of the sea that* **HANS** *floats in.*)

She feels her body expand and bubble up!

She floats atop the sea,

She crashes on the beach,

And she plays with the humans as they splash alongside her.

Being seafoam IS fun!

And then—

(**HANS** *emerges out of the sea as the rest of the cast builds the world of the sky.*)

She goes up!

Farther and farther

Higher and higher

Until she's way up above

Where the sky is as vast as the imagination.

(**HANS** *is a rain cloud.*)

(**HANS** *smiles as he looks at all the characters he's inspired around him.*)

And that's how the Little Mermaid lives a very fulfilling life

Being sometimes the rain, sometimes the sea.

(*Thunder. Lightning. Darkness.*)

(*The curtain call must be a jig. And when I say jig, I don't mean a mid-16th-century British folkdance. I mean a casually choreographed dance of jubilation set to pop music.**)

The End

---

* A license to produce *SOMETIMES THE RAIN, SOMETIMES THE SEA* does not include a performance license for any copyrighted music or recordings. Licensees should create their own. For further information, please see the Music and Third-Party Materials Use Note on page iii.

www.ingramcontent.com/pod-product-compliance
Ingram Content Group UK Ltd.
Pitfield, Milton Keynes, MK11 3LW, UK
UKHW021001130125
453657UK00012B/415